KIND

Written & Illustrated By:

Christine Reynebeau

Published by Dreambuilt Books
Printed in the USA.

Wausau, WI 54403

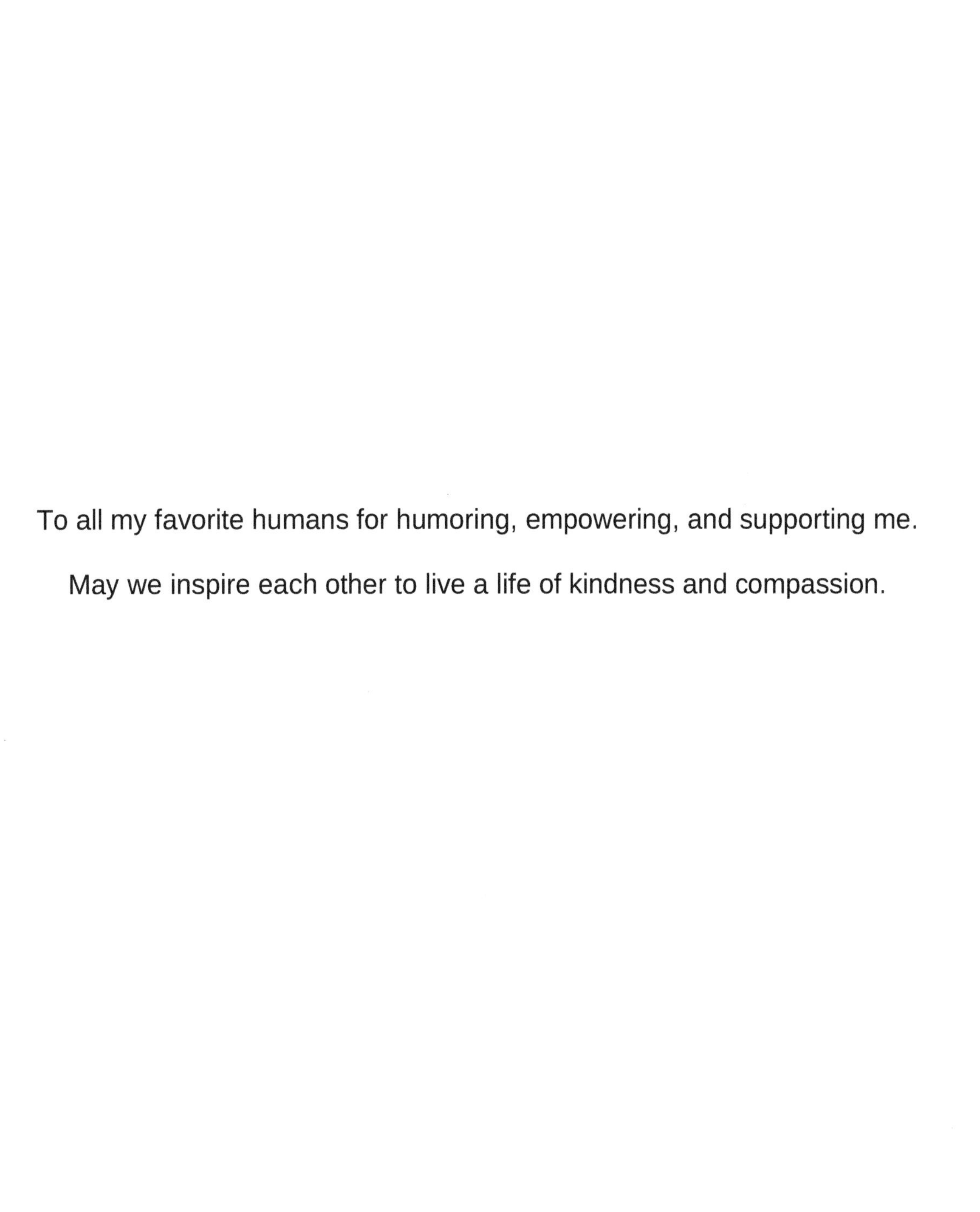

To all my favorite humans for humoring, empowering, and supporting me.

May we inspire each other to live a life of kindness and compassion.

We all went out at recess
in the cool, crisp fall.

All the kids started a big game of four-square with Lucy's new ball.

Lucy was winning;
the King square was her space,

When another ball flew out of
nowhere and hit her in the face.

It was Big Blair the Bully, the meanest girl in school.

Once she didn't like you, she'd pull your hair,

knock you down,

and make you
feel like a fool!

For the next few weeks, with every chance she had,

Big Blair would pick on Lucy until she was crying and sad.

One day, Lucy got home from school
and her eyes were filled with tears.

After she
explained it all,
her mom hugged
her tight,

And whispered in
her ear,

"You are stronger than you think; you are braver than you feel,"

"And all the sadness you feel
today, will absolutely heal,"

"The unkindness of others does not reflect on you, but the choices in how you react always do!"

"Many times your bully is being bullied too,"

"Or they're sad about something unknown to you."

"Choose forgiveness and compassion.
Choose to be kind."

Her mom hugged her again and sent her on her way,

And she kept her mom's words in
mind at school the next day!

She watched Big Blair spend free time alone,

Then she sat alone at lunch.

And when no one invited her to play at recess, she began to have a hunch.

So Lucy started a new game of four-square and invited Big Blair to play.

Even though everyone was nervous, Lucy encouraged Blair to stay.

They laughed and played until their cheeks were
red, from running in the sun.

Starting that day, Blair stopped being a bully and everyone had more fun!

The End